Go, Go Fish!

Dandi Daley Mackall

ILLUSTRATED BY

Elena Kucharik

Tommy NELSON®
www.tommynelson.com
A Division of Thomas Nelson, Inc.
www.ThomasNelson.com

Text copyright © 2001 by Dandi Daley Mackall
Illustrations copyright © 2001 by Elena Kucharik

Published in Nashville, Tennessee, by Tommy Nelson™,
a division of Thomas Nelson, Inc.

Library of Congress Cataloging-in-Publication Data

Mackall, Dandi Daley.
    Go, go, fish! / Dandi Daley Mackall; illustrated by Elena Kucharik.
        p. cm. – (I'm not afraid)
    Summary: A young fish is frightened by shadows, until the day it
encounters Jesus and learns not to be afraid.
    ISBN 0-8499-7751-7
    [1. Fishes—Fiction. 2. Fear of the dark—Fiction. 3. Jesus Christ—
Fiction. 4. Stories in rhyme.] I. Kucharik, Elena ill.

PZ8.3.M179 Go 2001
[E]—dc21

                                        2001042761

Printed in Singapore
01 02 03 04 05 TWP 5 4 3 2 1

In the darkest of depths of the Galilee Sea,
There I lived with a secret as deep as could be.
Known as Felipe Fish, I looked brave at first sight.
No one knew that this fish was afraid of the light.

Light makes shadows, I thought,
Spooky shapes on my fin.
I'll just swim way down here
Where no light will creep in.

Then along came a fish from a school at the top.
"Come on up!" called the fish. And before I could stop . . .
I was following, fast as a fish's fin flies!
'Cause he promised that nighttime had come to the skies.

So I swam to the surface, expecting the night.
Then I burst through the waters and saw a bright light!

There walked Jesus, the Christ, on the top of the sea!
Such a thing was unheard of in all Galilee!

Thunder boomed!
Lightning cracked as it streaked the black sky.
And I called out for help with a frightened fish cry.

Storm winds whipped the white waves, splashing, crashing a boat
That rocked over the crest, barely keeping afloat!

"I don't like this at all!" said that fish from the school.
"You can stay if you want. But not me! I'm no fool!"
All the fishermen watched as this Jesus drew near.
Though the other fish fled, I was frozen in fear.

As the white light grew closer, the next thing I knew,
On the water above me came Jesus' left shoe!

In His shadow I shivered and quivered afraid.
And I felt myself sinking. "Lord, save me!" I prayed.

"If you trust me," said Jesus, "there's nothing to fear."
I could sense as He said it, my fear disappear.
Then we looked to the heavens, the sailors and I,
To discover that Jesus had calmed the whole sky!

I will never forget what I learned on that night,
And I'll never again be afraid of the light.
So when you go to bed and they turn out the light,
Trust in Jesus to help, and he'll make it all right!